A NOTE TO PARENTS

When your children are ready to "step into reading," giving them the right books is as crucial as giving them the right food to eat. **Step into Reading Books** present exciting stories and information reinforced with lively, colorful illustrations that make learning to read fun, satisfying, and worthwhile. They are priced so that acquiring an entire library of them is affordable. And they are beginning readers with a difference—they're written on five levels.

Early Step into Reading Books are designed for brand-new readers, with large type and only one or two lines of very simple text per page. **Step 1 Books** feature the same easy-to-read type as the Early Step into Reading Books, but with more words per page. **Step 2 Books** are both longer and slightly more difficult, while **Step 3 Books** introduce readers to paragraphs and fully developed plot lines. **Step 4 Books** offer exciting nonfiction for the increasingly independent reader.

The grade levels assigned to the five steps—preschool through kindergarten for the Early Books, preschool through grade 1 for Step 1, grades 1 through 3 for Step 2, grades 2 through 3 for Step 3, and grades 2 through 4 for Step 4—are intended only as guides. Some children move through all five steps very rapidly; others climb the steps over a period of several years. Either way, these books will help your child "step into reading" in style!

For Chip
—C. G.

Text copyright © 1999 by Charles Ghigna.
Illustrations copyright © 1999 by Jon Goodell.
All rights reserved under International and Pan-American Copyright Conventions.
Published in the United States by Random House, Inc., New York, and simultaneously
in Canada by Random House of Canada Limited, Toronto.

www.randomhouse.com/kids

Library of Congress Cataloging-in-Publication Data
Ghigna, Charles.
Mice are nice / by Charles Ghigna ; illustrated by Jon Goodell.
    p.   cm. — (Step into reading. A step 1 book)
SUMMARY: Simple rhyming text extols the virtues of mice as the perfect pet.
ISBN 0-679-88929-9 (trade) — ISBN 0-679-98929-3 (lib. bdg.)
[1. Pets—Fiction. 2. Mice—Fiction. 3. Stories in rhyme.] I. Goodell, Jon, ill.
II. Title. III. Series: Step into reading. Step 1 book. PZ8.3.G345Mi 1999
[E]—dc21 98-27971

Printed in the United States of America 10 9 8 7 6 5 4 3 2 1

STEP INTO READING is a registered trademark and the Step into Reading colophon is a
trademark of Random House, Inc.

Step into Reading®

Mice Are Nice

by Charles Ghigna
illustrated by Jon Goodell

A Step 1 Book

Random House 🏠 New York

There are
many kinds of pets
at a pet store
called Babette's.

Bunnies, kittens,

parrots, puppies.

Ferrets, snakes,

and lots of guppies.

But if you want

the perfect pet,

mice are what

you need to get.

Because...

Ferrets smell.

Goldfish stare.

Birds drop feathers
everywhere!

Hound dogs howl
and yowl
and growl.

But mice are nice!

Mice are cuddly.

Mice are small.

Mice sleep curled up
in a ball.

Parrots chatter.
Kittens chase.

Puppies like to
lick your face.

Turtles hide
inside their shells
and stay...
all day!

But mice are nice!

Mice are gentle.

Mice are sweet.

Mice have tiny hands
and feet.

Dogs will chew
your favorite socks.

Cats will need
a litter box.

Boas squeeze.

Lizards shed.

Rabbits hide
beneath the bed.

But mice are nice!

Mice are soft.

Mice are sleek.

Mice like playing hide-and-seek!

Dogs jump fences.

Cats climb trees.

Both have fleas
and make you sneeze!

But mice are nice!

Mice can dart.

Mice can scurry.

Mice go places
in a hurry.

So if you want
the perfect pet,
mice are what
you need to get.

Because...

Mice can run

like a rocket.

Mice can fit...

...inside your pocket!

Yes, mice are nice!